The AmaZING adventures of JaCKDOG

Pizza delivery dog

E. Lynn Branch

Illustrations by
Blueberry Illustrations

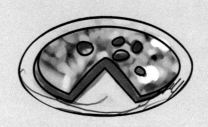

ISBN-13: 978-1547018864
ISBN-10: 1547018860

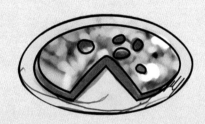

**For my Grandchildren
Iczaa, Jack, Jayleigh,
Kamille, Kherington,
Noah, Sayler & Taryn**

Jackdog is so excited! Today he has an appointment
with the owner of the Scratch N Sniff Pizza Parlor.
He is trying out for the Pizza Delivery Dog job.

"Take this pizza to 123 Beagle Boulevard right away!"
"Yes, sir!" says Jackdog.

Jackdog heads out on his very first pizza delivery.
Right away the delicious smell of the pizza fills the air.
Jackdog can't help but notice how great the pizza smells.
"I will eat just one small slice of pepperoni. I
am sure no one will notice," thinks Jackdog.

Jackdog begins eating the pepperoni slices and before he knows it, the last one is gone!

Before he knows it, the entire pizza is gone. Jackdog is now so scared of getting into trouble! He tries to think of a lie to tell Mr. Theodore.

I could say, "Aliens vaporized the pizza!"

Suddenly Jackdog remembers that when he was just a pup his parents had taught him to never tell a lie.

Jackdog is scared but he knows what he has to do. He rides back to the pizza parlor to tell Mr. Theodore the truth.

"I appreciate you telling the truth!" says Mr. Theodore. "As you told me the truth, I am going to give you another chance. Take this pizza to 456 Labrador Lane right away." "Yes, sir!" shouts Jackdog.

"Oh, this pizza smells so good!" Jackdog thinks again.

Jackdog can't take it anymore! He pulls to the side of the road and eats the pepperoni. Suddenly he feels terrible. "I have to do the right thing and deliver this pizza before I eat anymore!" he thinks.

Jackdog proudly makes the delivery.

Back at the Scratch N Sniff Pizza Parlor, Jackdog tells Mr. Theodore that he ate the pepperoni off that last pizza but he knows he can do better the next time.

"Please give me one more chance!" says Jackdog.

"Alright," says Mr. Theodore, "but this is your last chance." "Please take this pizza to 789 Poodle Pavilion."

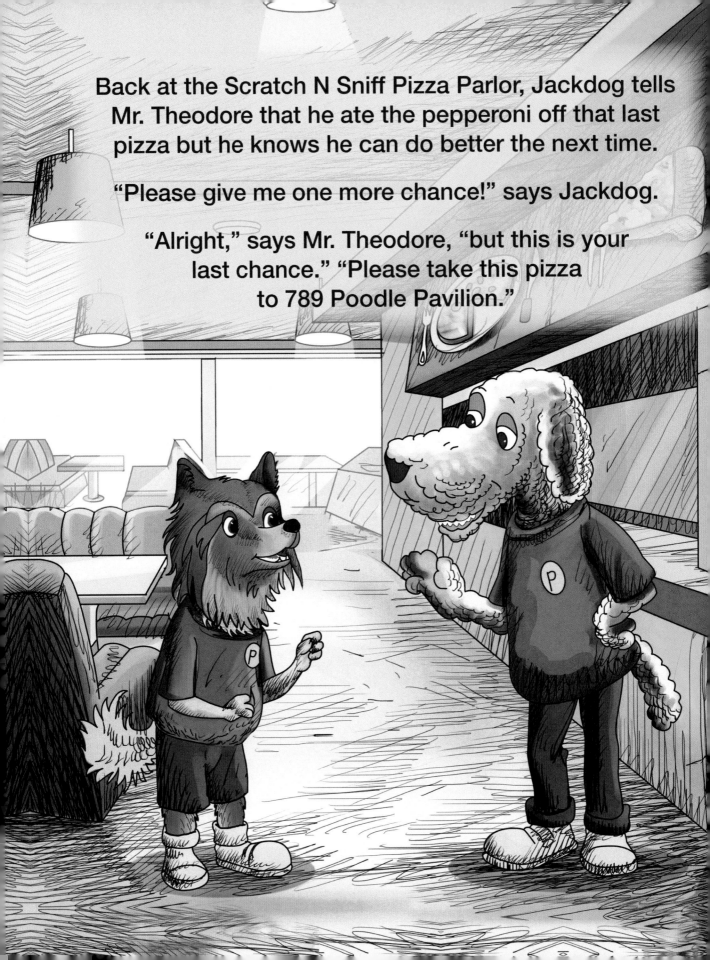

Jackdog immediately takes the pizza to the address. And although the pizza smells so delicious, he does not take a bite.

Jackdog returns and tells Mr. Theodore that he made the delivery. "Good job!" says Mr. Theodore. "I would like to offer you a full-time job as a pizza delivery dog!"

Just then Jackdog looked out the window and saw the cupcake delivery dog wanted sign. "Hmm, let me think about it!"

About the Author:

E. Lynn Branch is from Central California. She enjoys spending time with her children and grandchildren as well as her dogs and granddogs.

Made in the USA
Middletown, DE
14 October 2020